BO

AMERICA'S COMMANDER IN LEASH™

SECRETARY OF STATE

Naren Aryal
Illustrated by Danny Moore

Serving as America's Commander in Leash was such a thrill. I enjoyed roaming the halls of the White House, exploring the beautiful grounds, and spending time with the first family. I felt like the luckiest dog in the world!

Of course, being America's Commander in Leash came with official responsibilities, too. One day, President Obama called me from the Oval Office and asked me to lead a goodwill trip around the world. He said this would be a great opportunity for me to learn about foreign countries and cultures, while making new friends along the way.

"From America's Commander in Leash to America's Secretary of State! How does that sound, Bo?" President Obama joked.

I knew that the real Secretary of State was a very important advisor to the President and was responsible for knowing what was happening all around the world. With my tail wagging, I let the President know that I was ready for the adventure! "Good dog, Bo!" said the President.

Any United States Air Force aircraft carrying the President is known as "Air Force One."

Bo was born in Texas in 2008 and spent his first day in the White House on April 14, 2009.

After a warm send-off by the White House staff, I was ready to start my trip. With passport in paw, I was off to nearby Andrews Air Force Base where my journey would begin. The jumbo jet screamed down the runway, lifted high into the air, and headed over the Atlantic Ocean. I was on my way!

After a long flight over the Atlantic Ocean, I arrived in Ireland, my first stop. I traveled through the lush, green countryside on my way to Blarney Castle. I impressed a local gentleman with my bagpipe playing. "Top of the morning to you! Good dog, Bo!" he called.

From Ireland, it was a short trip to London, England. Before sightseeing, I enjoyed "fish and chips" with a friend. After filling my tummy, I hopped on a red double-decker bus and headed to Buckingham Palace. I thought the White House was big, but compared to this mansion, it was tiny! A British family spotted me and called, "Cheerio! Good dog, Bo!"

Buckingham Palace, home of the British Monarch, is about sixteen times larger than the White House.

Members of the Queen's Guard are best-known for their red coats, bear skin hats, and their ability to stand completely still while on duty.

My next stop was the Palace of Westminster and the clock tower known as "Big Ben." Checking the hands on the clock, I was reminded that it was time to hurry along to my next destination.

Portuguese water dogs were originally found along the coast of Portugal where they helped fishermen with their duties.

Staying in Europe, I headed to a charming seaside town along the Atlantic coast of Portugal. As you probably know, I'm a Portuguese water dog, so having the chance to visit the land of my ancestors, and finally learning how to swim, was a special treat. With the help of a swimming instructor, and a life jacket, I splashed into the ocean for lessons. In no time, I was swimming with the other dogs. "Olá! Good dog, Bo!" barked my new friends as I practiced doggy paddling.

Paris, France was nicknamed the "The City of Light" in the 1800s when it became the first city in Europe to light its streets with gas lamps.

My next stop was Paris, France, and the Eiffel Tower—one of the most famous landmarks in the world. Inspired by its beauty, I dressed like a Frenchman and painted a masterpiece. Excited to see my artwork, children approached me and said, "Bonjour! Good dog, Bo!"

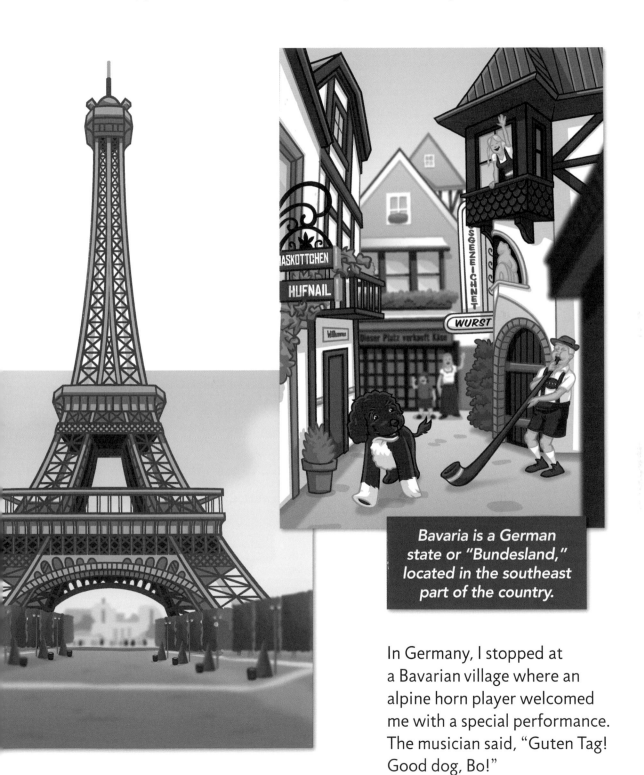

Bavaria is a German state or "Bundesland," located in the southeast part of the country.

In Germany, I stopped at a Bavarian village where an alpine horn player welcomed me with a special performance. The musician said, "Guten Tag! Good dog, Bo!"

The Roman Coliseum was built nearly 2,000 years ago and today is one of the most-visited tourist destinations in Italy.

Still in Europe, I visited Italy. In Rome, I toured the Coliseum and learned about the games and events this stadium hosted long ago. Dressed like a Roman Gladiator, I was ready for action!

At the Leaning Tower of Pisa, I posed for silly pictures while pretending to keep the tower from falling. "Watch out below!" hollered two of my fans.

The Leaning Tower of Pisa was designed to be straight, but soon after construction, it began tilting.

Since Italy is the birthplace of pizza, I decided to visit a local restaurant and try my paw at tossing pizza dough high into the air. I made the most delicious pizza ever...and the biggest mess ever!

At every stop, Italians were happy to see me. My new friends said, "Ciào! Good dog, Bo!"

Pizza originated in Italy, but today is one of the most popular food items in the world.

Next, I traveled to the continent of Africa. In Egypt, I couldn't wait to see the Great Pyramids of Giza where I ran into a very smart archeologist. He was excavating the site, looking for ancient artifacts. I toured the pyramids and admired the Great Sphinx with my new friend. I was amazed to learn how these structures were built so long ago.

From Egypt, I headed south to Kenya. At a lively Kenyan market, I picked up handmade gifts for friends back home. As I walked through the market, friends called, "Jambo! Good dog, Bo!"

President Obama's father was born in the East African country of Kenya.

The Serengeti, home to several national parks and wildlife reserves, is one of the most popular safari destinations in the world.

In Tanzania, I explored the Serengeti and came across amazing animals in their natural habitat. Being so close to these beautiful creatures was fun...but a little scary, too. Yikes! A lion roared, "Good dog, Bo!"

Located in Agra, India, the Taj Mahal was built by an emperor in memory of his beloved wife.

From Africa, I crossed the Indian Ocean on my way to India. In Agra, I visited the famous Taj Mahal. A nice couple gave me a tour of the majestic white-marble mansion. With their palms together and their heads bowed, the couple said, "Namaste! Good dog, Bo!"

Cricket was first played in England, but today is played in over one hundred countries, including India.

Next, an Indian cricket team invited me to join their match. I learned that cricket, like baseball, is played with a bat and ball. However, this game was nothing like baseball at all! After quickly learning the rules, I ran onto the field and helped my team to victory.

After working up a sweat, I was ready to cool off by trekking in the Himalayan Mountains of Nepal. With the help of a skilled mountain guide, I climbed Mount Everest, the tallest peak in the world. The guide said, "Good climbing, Bo!"

At an elevation of 29,035 feet above sea level, the peak of Mount Everest is the highest spot on Earth.

The Great Wall of China stretches over 4,000 miles and was built to protect the Chinese Empire.

China was my next stop. At the Great Wall of China, I marveled at the length of this structure. The wall stretched for miles...and miles...and miles. As I explored the wall, I came across a friendly Chinese family. Excited to see me, the family called, "Ni hao! Good dog, Bo!"

Chinese New Year is celebrated with festivals, feasts, family events, and fireworks.

Fortunately, I arrived in China during the Chinese New Year celebration. I watched beautiful parades wind down the streets of Beijing. Fireworks exploded overhead and everyone was having so much fun. I was greeted with calls of "Happy New Year, Bo!"

Over 30 million people call Tokyo home, making it the largest metropolitan area in the world.

From China, I continued to Japan. The streets of Tokyo were bustling with activity and packed with people. Everywhere I turned, I saw spectacular skyscrapers and crowds of people.

Located in Tokyo, Tsukiji fish market is the largest market in the world and offers over 400 types of seafood.

Excited to experience Japanese culture, I ventured over to the local fish market, where the day's catch was on display. Wow, I'd never seen such variety of fish all in one place. The market was really fun, but the fishy-smelling air took some getting used to!

Sumo is a Japanese form of wrestling in which the competitors attempt to force each other out of a ring.

In the evening, I watched a Sumo match, a favorite sport among the Japanese. Two large men displayed incredible strength and balance as they tried to push each other out of the ring. I thought the wrestlers' outfits were really funny! Noticing me nearby, the wrestlers said, "Konnichiwa! Good dog, Bo!"

Australia is an island, a country, and a continent.

From Japan, I made the long trip down under to Australia. In Sydney, I toured the world-famous Opera House. Inspired by the setting, I gave a performance for my Aussie fans. "Bravo! Good dog, Bo!" they cheered.

From the big city of Sydney, I made the journey to the Australian Outback. There, I viewed native wildlife and even met a group of Australia's Aboriginal people. One man welcomed me to the Outback by playing his didgeridoo.

Kangaroos, dingos, koalas, emus, and platypuses are all native to Australia.

The Great Barrier Reef was my next destination. I dove into the ocean to view the beautiful coral. Without disturbing the natural marine environment, I marveled at the colorful plants and the amazing variety of ocean life. A green sea turtle snapped, "G'day, mate! Good dog, Bo!"

The Great Barrier Reef is located along the northeast coast of Australia and is the world's largest coral reef system.

From Australia, I flew over the South Pacific Ocean all the way to South America. In Brazil, the United States soccer team happened to be in the country for a soccer match. Not wanting to miss an opportunity to help Team USA, I suited up for the match and I even scored the winning goal. My teammates cheered, "Goooaaaalll, Bo!"

I decided the best way to explore South America was by rafting down the mighty Amazon River. Along the way, people called, "Holà! Good dog, Bo!"

More water flows in the Amazon River than any other river in the world.

Soccer is the most popular sport in Brazil, South America's largest country.

My next stop took me south, all the way south, to Antarctica. While I didn't run into any people or dogs there, I did come across thousands of penguins. I waddled along with my new friends for a while, but it was just too cold for me. Brrrr! The penguins joked, "Chill out, Bo!"

Ice-covered Antarctica is home to penguins and seals, but no permanent human residents call the continent home.

Question: Can you guess how many miles Bo, America's Commander in Leash traveled in this book?

Answer: Approximately 49,000 miles!

After setting my paws on each of the seven continents and having the opportunity to meet so many nice people along the way, it was finally time for me to head back home. I packed up my things and made the long trip back to Washington, D.C.

What a great trip it had been! As I walked through the White House doors, the first family greeted me with hugs and pats. "Welcome home, Bo! We missed you!" said the first kids. I missed them, too!

After sharing pictures from my travels, I finally made it to my own cozy bed. As I drifted off to sleep, I thought about how lucky I was to be Bo, America's Commander in Leash.

Ireland

Start
Washington, D.C.

End

Portugal

Brazil

Antarctica

BO

AMERICA'S

COMMANDER IN LEASH

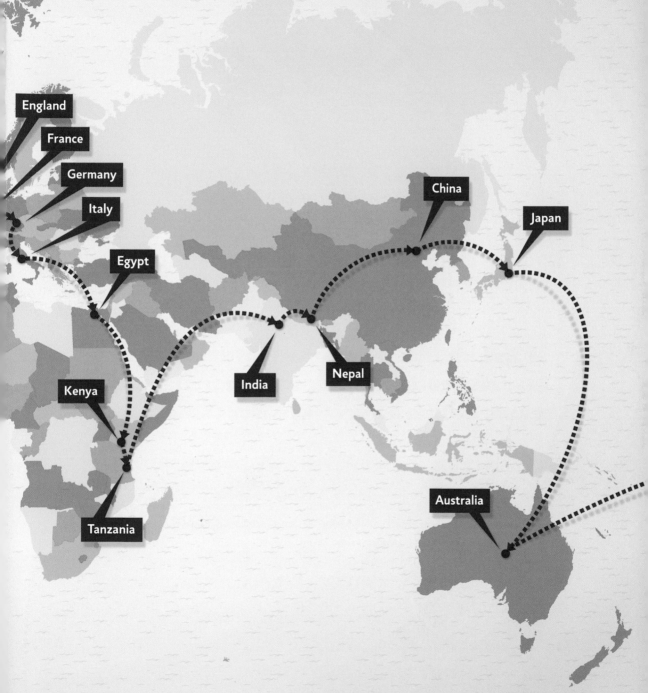

England

France

Germany

Italy

Egypt

China

Japan

Kenya

India

Nepal

Tanzania

Australia

For Anna, Maya, and the best pet in the world, Frenchie.
—Naren Aryal

This one goes out to Robie. Keep catching
those frisbees, and we'll keep throwing them.
—Danny Moore

**Contact Bo at bo@gooddogbo.com or
check him out online at www.GoodDogBo.com
Bo's Twitter page: GoodDogBo**

Find children's books featuring your favorite college and professional sports teams online at www.mascotbooks.com

For more information, please contact Mascot Books,
P.O. Box 220157, Chantilly, VA 20153-0157

ISBN: 1-934878-82-0
CPSIA Code: PRW0809A

Printed in the United States

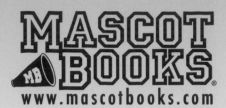